POLITICALLY CORRECT
HOLIDAY STORIES

POLITICALLY CORRECT
HOLIDAY STORIES

*For an Enlightened
Yuletide Season*

JAMES FINN GARNER

MACMILLAN • USA

MACMILLAN
A Simon & Schuster Macmillan Company
1633 Broadway
New York, NY 10019-6785

Copyright © 1995 by James Finn Garner

MACMILLAN is a registered trademark of Macmillan, Inc.

Interior illustrations by Lisa Amoroso
Interior design by Erich Hobbing

Library of Congress Cataloging-in-Publication Data available

ISBN 0-02-860420-2

Manufactured in the United States of America
10 9 8 7 6 5 4 3

Dedicated to the good persuns of Moorhead State University, where mistletoe has been officially banned as a holiday decoration, because, according to school president Roland Dille, it "tends to sanctify uninvited endearment."

Also, to Lies and Liam,
my shining Christmas stars.

CONTENTS

INTRODUCTION

Fluffy white snow. Cups of golden eggnog. Visions of sugar plums.

At this festive time of year, it is good for each and every one of us to consider carefully just how cruel and exclusionary so many of our old seasonal "traditions" continue to be. To place so much emphasis on snowfalls and a "White Christmas" surely is a slap in the face for those persuns in developing tropical nations, who never get to see snow firsthand. The friendly offer of a cup of eggnog is nothing less than a poke in the eye to the dedicated vegans among us. And anyone recovering from an eating disorder can certainly attest that visions of sugar plums dancing in one's head are more like a nightmare than a sweet dream.

Because of the callousness and insensitivity that abound during the holiday season, I felt compelled once again to perform a public service in the name of right-thinking celebrants everywhere and revise the favorite seasonal tales for our more sensitive era.

To avoid any suggestion that with this book I am cashing in on the holiday's consumer feeding frenzy, let me mention that I tried to persuade my publisher to bring this volume out at a more sedate time of year, such as February or March, when everyone could discuss these emerging ideas calmly and rationally. But the book was made ready for autumn publication because we agreed that one more old-fashioned holiday season is one too many.

To all those cynics who believe that a responsible and progressive celebration must also be differently enjoyable (i.e., no fun), I would ask them to consider the evolution of current traditions. We are all aware (or should be) that the early Christians chose to celebrate the birth of their savior at the same time as pagan winter festivals that welcomed the return of the sun. They were thus able to celebrate "Christ's mass" without alienating their neighbors and doubled their chances of being invited to a tasty feast at the same time. Such an early example of inclusionary merrymaking should inspire us all. Today's neopagans can feel especially proud of their heritage/himitage.

We can also turn the holidays into opportunities for positive critical thinking by taking instruction from many legends and oral traditions. Consider the senior lifemate's tale about the animals imprisoned in the barnyard, who are granted the gift of speech on Christmas Eve. Initially we might look on this as a disturbing attempt to anthropomorphize other species, forcing them against their will to celebrate the holidays of human animals at the neglect of their own traditions. However, we can turn this fable into an exercise in positive self-reflection if we try to imagine the insights the animals might reveal to us about our own species. Whether we like what they have to tell us, of course, is another matter.

It is certainly regrettable that this task of liberating the holidays from the oppressiveness of tradition has not been undertaken before, and that it has been left up to a member of my race, class, and gender to complete. To employ the symbols of the season, I do not consider myself a wise man, a shining star, a lamp of miraculous oil, a feast of first fruits, a heavenly messenger, a piñata, or any type of magickal log or fiery pudding. I hope to avoid any impression that I pattern myself after that other member of the Genital Power Elite, Kris Kringle, barging in and assuming that my "gifts" will be gratefully accepted by right-thinking persuns everywhere. My only wish is that you will enjoy these stories and share them with your family, alternative household, or other social or non-social group. I hope they will become a new tradition for you, at least until something better comes along. And may your holidays be whatever you decide to make them, if indeed you make them anything at all.

'TWAS THE NIGHT BEFORE SOLSTICE

T was the night before solstice and all
through the co-op
Not a creature was messing the calm
status quo up.

The children were nestled all snug in their beds,
Dreaming of lentils and warm whole-grain breads.

We'd welcomed the winter that day after school
By dancing and drumming and burning the Yule,

A more meaningful gesture to honor the planet
Than buying more trinkets for Mom or Aunt Janet,

Or choosing a tree just to murder and stump it
And dress it all up like a seasonal strumpet.

My lifemate and I, having turned down the
   heat,
Slipped under the covers for a well-deserved
   sleep,

When from out on the lawn there came such a
   roar
I fell from my futon and rolled to the floor.

I crawled to the window and pulled back the latch,
And muttered, "Aw, where is that Neighborhood
   Watch?"

I saw there below through the murk of the night
A sleigh and eight reindeer of nonstandard height.

At the reins of that sleigh sat a mean-hearted
   knave
Who treated each deer like his persunal slave.

I'd seen him before in some ads for car loans,
Plus fast food and soft drinks and cellular phones.

He must have cashed in from his mercantile chores,
Since self-satisfaction just oozed from his pores.

He called each by name, as if he were right
To treat them like humans, entrenching his might:

"Now Donder, now Blitzen," and other such aliases,
Showing his true Eurocentrical biases.

With a snap of his fingers, away they all flew,
Like lumberjacks served up a plate of tofu.

Up to the rooftop they carried the sleigh
(The holes in the shingles are there to this day).

Out bounded the man, who went straight to the flue.
I knew in an instant just what I should do.

After donning my slippers, downstairs did I dash
To see this trespasser emerge from the ash.

His clothes were all covered with soot, but of
  course,
From our wood-fueled alternative energy source.

Through the grime I distinguished the make of his
  duds—
He was dressed all in fur, fairly dripping with blood.

"We're a cruelty-free house!" I proclaimed with
   such heat
He was startled and tripped on the logs at his feet.

He stood back up dazed, but with mirth in
   his eyes.
It was then that I noticed his unhealthy size.

He was almost as wide as when standing erect,
A lover of fatty fried foods, I suspect.

But that wasn't all to make sane persuns choke:
In his teeth sat a pipe that was belching out smoke!

I could scarcely believe what invaded our house.
This carcinogenic and overweight louse

Was so red in the face from his energy spent,
I expected a heart attack right there and then.

Behind him he toted a red velvet bag
Full to exploding with sinister swag.

He asked, "Where is your tree?" with a face
   somewhat long.
I said, "Out in the yard, which is where it belongs."

"But where will I put all the presents I've brought?"
I looked at him squarely and said, "Take the lot

"To some frivolous people who think that they need
To succumb to the sickness of commerce and greed,

"Whose only joy comes from the act of consuming,
Thus sending the stock of the retailers booming."

He blinked and said, "Ho, ho, ho! But you're
    kidding."
I gave him a stare that was stern and forbidding.

"Surely children need something with which to have
    fun?
It's like childhood's over before it's begun."

He looked in my eyes for some sign of assent,
But I strengthened my will and refused to relent.

"They have plenty of fun," I cut to the gist,
"And your mindless distractions have never been
    missed.

"They take CPR so that they can save lives,
And go door-to-door for the used clothing drives.

"They recycle, renew, reuse—and reveal
For saving the planet a laudable zeal.

"When they padlock themselves to a fence to protest
Against nuclear power, we think they're the best."

He said, "But they're children—lo, when do they
     play?"
I countered, "Is that why you've driven your sleigh,

"To bring joy to the hearts of each child and tot?
All right, open your bag; let's see what you've
     got."

He sheepishly did as I'd asked and behold!
A Malibu Barbie in a skirt made of gold.

"You think that my girls will like playing with
     this,
An icon of sexist, consumerist kitsch?

"With its unnatural figure and airheaded grin,
This trollop makes every girl yearn to be thin,

"And take up fad diets and binging and purging
Instead of respecting her own body's urging

6

"To welcome the shape that her body has found
And rejoice to be lanky, short, skinny, or round."

Deep in his satchel he searched for a toy,
Saying, "This is a hit with most little boys."

And what did he put in my trembling hand
But a gun from the BrainBlasters Power Command!

"It's a 'hit,' to be sure," I sneered in his face,
"And a plague to infect the whole human race!

"How 'bout grenades or some working bazookas
To turn *all* of our kids into half-wit palookas?"

I seized on his bag just to see for myself
The filth being spread by this odious elf.

An Easy-Bake Oven—ah, goddess, what perfidy!
To hoodwink young girls into household captivity!

Plus an archery play set with shafts that fly out,
The very thing needed to put your eye out.

And toy metal tractors, steam shovels, and cranes
For tearing down woodlands and scarring the plains,

Plus "games" like Monopoly, Pay Day, Tycoon,
As if lessons in greed can't start up too soon.

And even more weapons from BrainBlasters Co.,
Like cannons and nunchucks and ray guns that glow.

That's all I could find in his red velvet sack—
Perverseness and mayhem to set us all back.

(But I did find one book that caused me to
    ponder—
Some fine bedtime tales by a fellow named
    Garner.)

"We need none of this," I announced in a huff,
"No 'business-as-usual' holiday stuff.

"We sow in our offspring more virtue than this.
Your 'toys' offer some things they never will
    miss."

The big man's expression was a trifle bereaved
As he shouldered his pack and got ready to leave.

"I pity the kids who grow up around here,
Who're never permitted to be of good cheer,

"Who aren't allowed leisure for leisure's own sake,
But must fret every minute—it makes my heart
    break!"

"Enough histrionics! Don't pity our kids
If they don't do as Macy's or Toys 'R' Us bids.

"They live by their principles first and foremost
And know what's important," to him did I boast.

"Pray, could I meet them?" "Oh no, they're not here.
They're up on the roof, liberating your deer!"

Then Santa Claus sputtered and pointed his finger
But, mad as he was, he had no time to linger.

He flew up the chimney like smoke from a fire,
And up on the roof I heard voices get higher.

I ran outside the co-op to see him react
To my children's responsible, kindhearted act.

He chased them away, and disheartened, dismayed,
He rehitched his reindeer (who'd docilely stayed).

I watched with delight as he scooted off then.
He'd be too embarrassed to come back again.

But with parting disdain, do you know what he said,
When this overweight huckster took off in his sled?

This reindeer enslaver, this exploiter of elves?
"Happy Christmas to all, but get over yourselves!!"

FROSTY
THE PERSUN
OF SNOW

obby and Betty were two siblings who fought over everything. Sometimes they fought over big things, sometimes they fought over little things (and as with most male/female conflict communication patterns, they usually couldn't even agree on which issues were big and which were little). No amount of crisis intervention could get them to stop bickering.

One winter day, their frustrated caregiver sent them outside to play. A layer of fresh snow had fallen the previous night, the first of the season, and the world outside looked as heavily frosted as a matrimonial enslavement cake. As everything around them glistened, Bobby and Betty tried to agree on what games to play.

Should they make a snow fort? Too militaristic, said Betty.

How about snow angels? No, countered Bobby, they had been raised agnostic. Besides, such a public display of religious figures might make others uncomfortable.

And so it was with sledding, skating, and snowball fights—all were rejected for one reason or another. Then Betty suggested that they create people out of snow. Try as he might, Bobby couldn't find anything wrong in his sister's idea, so they each started to roll the biggest snowballs they could. Then they set these on top of each other for a body. Betty rolled a smaller snowball for a head and lifted it high atop the other two. They used two twigs to give it arms, and two lumps of coal and a button to give it a face. Bobby wanted to put a corncob pipe in its mouth, but Betty objected, saying the implied endorsement would harm the more impressionable children in the neighborhood.

Bobby said angrily, "When I make a snowman, he always has a corncob pipe!"

"What do you mean?" Betty answered. "This was my idea, and I say it's a snowwommon!"

"But it's *shaped* like a man!" said Bobby.

"Only to a phallocentric world view like yours!" said Betty.

"How can it be a wommon if we use the old top hat? Womyn don't wear top hats!"

"Oh yeah? What about Marlene Dietrich?"

And so it continued, with neither side budging an inch and the snow figure standing there, a silent witness. In a snit, Bobby decided to show his sibling that it was indeed a masculine snow individual, and slammed the hat on top of its head.

As soon as he did so, a quick gust of wind blew about them, and snow crystals spun around and around like a frigid tornado. Then, as suddenly as it had started, the wind settled down. Bobby and Betty wiped the snow from their eyes. They were about to resume their argument when an innocent voice asked, "What's all the fuss about?"

The siblings stopped and turned to the source of the voice. There, right where they had just assembled their frigid figure, stood a living, breathing, and fully articulate snow being! Their mouths fell open as they stared at this marvel.

"It seems like such a silly argument," it continued, "especially since you neglected to give me any private parts."

Betty regained her composure quickly. "I don't care if you *were* born only an instant ago," she said. "How can you be so naive as to think a persun's gender is determined by their physical equipment? It's a cultural issue first and foremost."

"If you want to get huffy," retorted the newcomer, "tell me why you were going to assign me a gender without asking me my preference first."

Betty's face reddened at her insensitivity.

"So what would you prefer?" asked Bobby.

"After watching the way you two communicate, I prefer neither. I think I'd like to be called a 'persun of snow.'"

"And what should your name be?" asked Betty, trying to make amends.

"In a post-modern comment on the preconceptions of society at large, I'm going to choose the most obvious name possible. You can call me 'Frosty'!"

Bobby and Betty agreed that it was a wonderful name. The arrival of their new friend was so magickal and exciting that the children completely forgot their earlier argument. Frosty and the pre-adults danced and played and laughed together for hours, with nary a cross word between the siblings.

As the sun climbed in the sky, the children continued to scamper about, but Frosty began to feel wet and heavy. Soon the persun of snow was having a difficult time keeping up with the pre-adults.

"What's the matter, Frosty?" they asked with concern.

"Oh, it's so hot!" Frosty said. "I'm not made of flesh and blood like you. If the temperature keeps rising, soon there will be nothing left of me."

"The Earth's getting warmer, due to the depletion of the ozone layer," said Bobby matter-of-factly. "We learned all about it at Montessori school."

"The ozone layer?" repeated Frosty. "I don't know what that is, but we better do something about it fast, or I'll turn into a puddle of water."

"How about a march on Washington?" suggested Betty.

"Yes, that's exactly the thing!" said her brother.

"Then let's hurry," said Frosty. "If enough of us march, the government will *have* to take action."

Frosty ran through the neighborhood, mobilizing the rest of the snow citizens. In backyards and front yards, in parks and in playgrounds, snow persuns of every size and shape listened to Frosty's plan. The magick from its top hat and the passion in its speech enabled them all to throw off the icy chains of passivity and take positive action for their own survival. Soon the charismatic Frosty had gathered a good-sized crowd, ready to take their argument to the government.

Bobby and Betty did their part as well. They rounded up their dog Spot and their kitty Puff and prepared to head off. Then they called their friends Ahmout and Fatima, and their friends Ho-shi and Chin-wa, and their friends Shadrach and Lu'Minaria, and their friend Heather and her two mommies, and the whole crowd joined in with the march of the persuns of snow.

Frosty walked at the head of the parade, holding a broomstick high. Others carried signs with messages like "No Ozone = No-Snow Zone" and "We Won't Just Melt Away!" En route to Washington, they picked up other supporters, snow and non-snow alike. Frosty and friends also got the attention of the media, since the sight of the Rubenesque, dark-eyed snowpersuns made such "great TV" for the video crews.

Soon the marchers made it to the Capitol Mall, where they were determined to camp until the president agreed to meet and hear their concerns. Where the icy protestors gathered, the mall looked as if it were covered with a plush white carpet, with tiny clusters of humans tossed on it like colorful stones. Unfortunately, Washington did not have a cool climate at all, and many of the persuns of snow were beginning to feel very uncomfortable.

It wasn't long before the news finally came: The vice president had agreed to speak with Frosty on television, in a remote one-on-one discussion about the steps needed to halt ozone breakdown. Excitement rippled through the encampment on the mall. Finally their concerns would be taken seriously!

A camera crew came later that day and set up the chairs, monitors, and cameras that would be needed. Bobby and Betty were particularly excited for Frosty, who was by now a dear friend. Ever since Frosty's arrival, in fact, the children had scarcely quarreled at all. Betty hugged Frosty around the neck and said, "We're so proud of you!"

"Aw, thanks," said Frosty, "but I haven't done

much of anything yet. You should be proud of how everyone got together—snow and skin alike—and worked to protect the environment. Now please listen carefully. If anything should ever happen to me, I hope you two will be able to stop fighting once and for all and lead the movement in my place."

Bobby and Betty promised their friend to do their best.

It was time for the broadcast to begin. The TV people tried to put some makeup on Frosty, to cut down on the glare off its forehead, but soon realized the task was impossible. Frosty sat in the appointed chair and waited for the director's signal.

Suddenly the lights went on and the sign was given that they were on the air. Out of respect for the office, Frosty let the vice president give the opening remarks. As the politician talked, the persun of snow began to feel very warm and sluggish. When the vice president was through, Frosty tried to state the marchers' position firmly, but the persun of snow was feeling so tired that it paused often and had trouble catching its breath. As time went on, Frosty slumped in the chair, looking worse and worse. By the time Bobby and Betty screamed, "Stop! Turn off the lights!" it was too late. On national television, under the glare of the hot lights, Frosty had melted irrevocably into a gray pile of slush.

Bobby and Betty were very sad for their friend, as were the rest of the protestors. But in the end, its demise was not tragic at all. Frosty had dramatized the plight of the ozone layer in a way that a squadron of scientists could never have. Everyone watching television that day was deeply moved by Frosty's brave sacrifice. Switchboards at the White House and the Capitol were lit up for hours, and within weeks new guidelines were established for both industry and government agencies to reduce the emissions that were eating away at the ozone.

Bobby and Betty took Frosty's top hat and went home. They tried to do as Frosty said and stop squabbling, but without their friend's calming influence, it was very hard for them. Their very different ideas about how to honor Frosty's memory and keep the movement alive couldn't be reconciled. As the weather got warmer, they moved on to other arguments and began to forget about their wintry friend. The next year, when they tried to recapture the magick of that first snowfall, they were unable to find Frosty's top hat and had to settle for making persuns of snow who faced their fates silently and unflinchingly.

THE NUTCRACKER

nce, many Christmas Eves ago, Clara's parents were throwing a party for their many friends and relations. These festive gatherings were an annual event in Clara's household, a singular opportunity during the year for everyone to forget their cares, to dance and gossip, and to eat as many fatty and sugary foods as possible. (Clara's parents felt it best to get such impulses out of one's system on a regular basis.) For the children, the chef would always bake a large gingerbread castle, wonderfully decorated with scores of marzipan peasants and serfs scaling the walls and overthrowing the parasitical king and his family.

These parties were always a joy for Clara and her brother Fritz because they meant presents, especially presents from their Uncle Drosselmeier. Their uncle was a mysterious, out-of-the-mainstream sort of chap, whose alternative lifestyle (if indeed he even had a lifestyle) was the subject of much speculation. He was gaunt of face and wore a gargantuan powdered wig and a patch over one eye ("Mostly for effect," said Clara's father). He was predisposed dramatic gestures and exotic, ostentatious clothing—anything to shake up people's bourgeois complacency. But Clara and Fritz loved their charismatic relative, both for his independent attitude and for the marvelously intricate mechanical toys he built for them.

On this Christmas Eve, their uncle arrived later than usual, but the delay merely heightened the excitement of his arrival. It wasn't until after the guests had gorged themselves on dinner that he finally appeared in the main hall with a sack over his shoulder. Clara, Fritz, and the other children could barely contain their delight, and nearly knocked Uncle Drosselmeier down to see what he'd brought this year.

Their uncle snickered cryptically, then reached into his bag with a great flourish. The adults as well as the pre-adults gathered round him in curiosity.

The man of augmented eccentricity smiled at all the attention and pulled out a silver top, decorated with intriguing symbols.

"To make holiday gift-giving more inclusive and outreaching," he said in a quavery voice, "I have developed this, the world's first automatic dreidel." He set this marvel on the tabletop, where it began to spin on its own power, glittering and gleaming and whirring. When it finally began to slow down and fell on its side, it made a strange clicking sound, then spit coins out of a small slit near its handle.

Everyone gasped and clapped their hands at this mechanical wonder, except for a few spoilsports who complained that children were forgetting how to entertain themselves with all these new automatic playthings. Next from his satchel Uncle Drossel-meier pulled out a doll, which looked ordinary enough after the spectacular dreidel. He smirked at everyone's apparent disappointment, then turned a knob in the doll's back. "Momma . . . " said the doll in a natural-sounding voice, "or Poppa . . . whichever caregiver is available."

The crowd thought this was quite ingenious and also socially progressive. He presented the doll to his niece, who handled it gingerly. Then from the bag, he pulled out the final gift: a hand-carved Nutcracker, dressed as a soldier and wearing the most comical expression. He handed this little figure to Fritz.

Oh, was there a hue and cry at this! It was bad enough to reinforce gender roles by handing Clara the doll, but on top of that, to give young, impressionable Fritz such an obvious symbol of castration and emasculation was inexcusable! People grew so angry that Uncle Drosselmeier feared he would be forcibly ejected from the party.

"I intended no harm," he protested sincerely. "I meant for the children to share the toys equally." He then swapped the doll and the Nutcracker between Clara and Fritz. (Years later, this incident, among others, would come back to Fritz while he underwent repressed-memory therapy, much to the chagrin and legal entanglement of his well-meaning uncle.)

Clara liked the Nutcracker and played with it for the rest of the evening. The guests ate and drank long into the night, giving not a thought to the purging and colonic irrigation that would be necessary the next morning. After they had all left, Clara's father tried to persuade her it was time for bed.

"Please may I stay up a while longer?" she asked. "The Nutcracker is telling me stories about why he left the military."

Her father smiled wearily and walked upstairs. Some time later, Clara set the Nutcracker on the cupboard shelf just as the clock struck midnight. As the final chime rang, very strange things began to happen in the room. Through the floor and out of the baseboards came a crowd of squeaking, scurrying mice—hundreds of mice, an entire army of mice! And in their midst stood their leader, a multi-craniumed Mouse King, who wore a golden crown on each of his seven heads.

Clara was marvelling at this when she heard the toys in the cupboard begin to stir and shout. "Oh, help," they cried. "The Mouse King and his expansionist forces have returned! Oh, save us, Nutcracker! Lead us into battle!"

To Clara's utter amazement, her little friend the Nutcracker walked forward and addressed them all: "Good citizens, think for a minute. Do you really want to perpetuate the old 'Great Man' myth of history/herstory? Important actions arise from the will of the people, not from the megalomania of any one individual!"

The toys admitted that their first impulse had been a tad servile and reactionary. They formed a committee to examine possible action plans to counter the Mouse King's advances. They then appointed the Nutcracker to head a fact-finding and cultural-interchange team to develop a dialog with the mice.

The fact-finding team headed out and returned twenty minutes later, tattered and bloodied. The toys then voted to assemble a crisis intervention team, again with the Nutcracker at the helm. This team headed out and returned fifteen minutes later, in even worse shape than the first. It seemed their non-aggressive options were dwindling.

After much debate, the toys agreed on their final course of action: They would send out a team of mediators to negotiate a peaceful settlement to the current crisis. Despite his now-tattered appearance, the Nutcracker was again chosen to lead the delegation. With the blessings and hopes of the other toys and Clara, the team went forth. Twenty minutes passed with no word, then an hour, then ninety minutes. Finally, after two anxious hours, the mediators returned with joyful news.

"We have an agreement with the Mouse King," announced the Nutcracker. "If we will help them liberate food from the pantry regularly, they will retreat from the territory they currently occupy." The toys let out a cheer and hailed the mediation team for their wisdom and hard work.

The Nutcracker walked over to Clara, who had stayed to lend her support to the beleaguered toys. "The Mouse King wasn't nearly so dangerous and irrational as he seemed," explained the wooden individual. "I finally deduced from his seven-headed appearance that he might be suffering from some sort of multiple-persunality disorder, which made him delusional and paranoid. Once I made contact with the most rational and judicious of his persunalities, we easily reached an accord."

"Bravo!" cried Clara. "Your dedication is to be praised. Mice certainly have been feared and marginalized for much too long."

The Nutcracker made a mannerly bow. "And now, sweet Clara, I would like to take you on a journey to my own kingdom, through the Christmas Wood and the Glade of the Sugar Plum Fairies, to the capital of Toyland, the wondrous Candytown!"

Clara was surprised by his offer. "I-I'm sorry," she stammered, "but . . . no."

The Nutcracker was crestfallen, and his larger-than-average jaw dropped to his chest.

"You see, we've been discussing just this sort of idea in our Storybook Womyn's Study Group," explained Clara. "We object that it's always the young womyn who are forced to undertake these disruptive journeys. The obvious implication is that we are all docile, helpless, and easily manipulated, and that our backgrounds and identities are of lesser importance. And even you should be able to see how such a journey is symbolic of the violent abduction that occurs on the wedding night. So, in memory of Dorothy and of Alice—poor, poor Alice; she's never regained her grip on reality, you know—I have to decline."

The Nutcracker felt a bit foolish after this. Unaware of the symbolism of his invitation, he certainly had intended no disrespect. He excused himself in the most courteous manner and gathered all the toys together again in the cupboard. The last thing Clara remembered before waking up was the Nutcracker's courtly bow, which she accepted with the graciousness with which it was offered.

The next morning, Clara found herself curled up on the floor of the drawing room, next to the toy cupboard. Inside she could see all the toys in their usual places, and in the middle of them all, the Nutcracker—immobile, steadfast, and still smiling. "What a wonderful, peace-loving dream!" she said to herself. "Yet not so much a dream as an attainable reality."

Clara stretched and rose from the carpet. As she looked around the room in the early morning light, her happiness was tempered by a pitiful scene. On the table in the dining room sat the ruins of the gingerbread castle, which had been sacked and destroyed by mice while she dreamt during the night.

RUDOLPH THE NASALLY EMPOWERED REINDEER

he story of Rudolph is a familiar one to most of the pre-adults in America and other parts of the Western world (not that this fact is an endorsement of Western culture, just an acknowledgment that the publicity and merchandising machines run more efficiently in those areas). While the image of an eager young reindeer cheerfully giving his all for

Santa Claus might be useful to department stores and jingle writers, the truth of his story is more complicated.

It's true that from birth Rudolph was a unique individual, that his luminescent olfactory organ made him different from (but not inferior to) the other reindeer in his age category, and that they often maliciously taunted him about his supra-nasal capabilities. Some reindeer caregivers, concerned that his nose had resulted from radioactive fallout or was somehow contagious, warned their fawns not to play with him.

What is *not* true is that Rudolph was disappointed to be so ostracized. While his parents successfully fought to have him schooled alongside the other young bucks and does, Rudolph always fancied himself an outsider. In fact, he worked to cultivate his image as an "angry young reindeer." He had no interest in the other reindeer and their inane games. He took himself and his fluorescent gift seriously and was convinced he had a higher calling in this life: to improve the fortunes of the working reindeer and overthrow the oppressive tyranny of Santa Claus.

For untold years, the success of Santa's toy-making monopoly depended on the co-option and exploitation of both the reindeer and elf populations. To this end, his most important criteria for the reindeer in his team were strong legs, a ten-point rack, and minimal gray matter. (The fact that he only recruited bucks for his team and excluded the does is cause for more outrage—Santa insisted it was to protect the morale of the enlisted bucks—but unfortunately, in Rudolph's time, the does were still awaiting their liberatrix.)

To Santa, Rudolph was one of the Northland's most dangerous creatures: a reindeer with a brain. He had seen a few during his years at the Pole, but there was something about Rudolph that made him especially nervous. It might have been the deer's standoffish attitude, or the rumors that he was organizing meetings with the other reindeer late at night. Santa also sensed a charisma in Rudolph that, if not kept in proper check, might disrupt his tidy little enterprise.

And so it was that, on that fabled foggy evening, Santa found himself in a bind. Harsh weather conditions left him unable to exploit the aerodynamic talents of his team. He had of course flown them through all sorts of dangerous weather before, with no thought to the deer's physical strain or mental trauma. But on this night the weather was so tempestuous that the bearded slave driver was fearful for his own safety and for the insurance headaches that a crash at his own toy works would certainly create.

Although Santa had known for years about Rudolph's gift for incandescent dissemination, he had not called special attention to it. In due time, Santa selfishly calculated, a use for it would arise, and until then there was no need to tip off how valuable Rudolph's skill might prove to be. That moment had finally arrived. On that foggy night, he sought out Rudolph among the herd and, wearing his humblest and most pleading face, asked him, "Rudolph, with your nose so bright, won't you guide my sleigh tonight?"

The young reindeer looked him over carefully. After a few moments of silence, he said, "No."

Santa blinked a few times and repeated, "No?" The herd could scarcely believe its ears as well.

"No. Not without concessions," replied the creature who happened to be antlered. "The days when we jump every time you whistle are over."

"What are you talking about, concessions?" blustered Santa, who hadn't planned on this twist. "This is your big break, your chance to join the team. This is the life's dream of every young reindeer."

Rudolph laughed. "This is starting to sound like *A Star Is Born*. Next you're going to tell me, 'Kid, you're going out there a nervous young buck, but you're coming back . . . a star.'"

The herd all chuckled at this remark. Perhaps such a gung-ho speech was all too familiar to them. Santa reddened, realizing he'd made a tactical error in approaching this young firebrand in public. He said, "It's cold out here. Why don't we talk this over inside my chalet. I have some very good moss and lichens, just picked . . . "

"I'll eat what everyone else eats," countered Rudolph, "and whatever you have to say to me, you can say out here." The other reindeer were watching this face-off with great interest. For years, they had treated Rudolph with suspicion for all his bold ideas, but now he was bravely sticking up for them at the expense of his own career. Some shouted encouragement, while the more reactionary deer grumbled about not rocking the kayak.

Santa began to feel some pressure as the minutes ticked away and the fog grew thicker. Finally he asked Rudolph what his demands were.

"You work the reindeer too hard, with no consideration for our families," Rudolph said. "We want a guarantee of no work on holidays."

For the next thirty minutes Santa tried to explain the disadvantages of this idea, the main one being, of course, that the reindeer only worked one night a year anyway, and since that night *always* fell on a holiday, such a change would make their jobs (and his) rather difficult to fulfill. Rudolph eventually agreed to table the issue for the time being.

Checking his watch, Santa was starting to sweat, even in the Arctic cold. "Could we speed this up?" he asked. "Or maybe forge a temporary working agreement that we can make permanent after Christmas?"

Rudolph snorted in his face. "We weren't born yesterday, Claus. No contract, no flight. If Christmas doesn't come this year, who do you think the children will blame? The reindeer? The weather? The Interstate Commerce Commission? No, they'll blame the overfed guy in the red suit."

Santa imagined the public relations headaches this would cause him, and his frame began to sag. Rudolph grilled him on such issues as health care, paternity leave, profit sharing, and joint decision-making councils. As the fog refused to lift and the minutes ticked away, Santa granted more and more of the deer's demands.

In the end, Rudolph and the reindeer rank-and-file could claim a number of victories: The deer would be required to fly only one night a year, and after four hours on the job, they would receive a ninety-minute dinner break and three fifteen-minute breaks. Santa was required to keep four alternate reindeer on standby for the duration of Christmas Eve at full pay and benefits. In addition, the mandatory retirement age was lowered to eight years, after which the reindeer were to receive a full pension and lifetime health care.

After all the terms were finalized, an exhausted but relieved Santa Claus hitched Rudolph up with the rest of the team. The other deer gave Rudolph three cheers for standing up for their rights against "the man," which the nasally empowered reindeer, feeling fulfilled for the first time, gratefully accepted. Using his unique luminescent gift, he led the sleigh through the inhospitable weather and Christmas that year was saved.

EPILOGUE

Like the fabled prophet in his own land, however, Rudolph found his real influence evaporating soon after that. For weeks he was praised by all the other reindeer, who told him, "You'll go down in history/herstory!" All the attention and admiration, however, began to feel superficial and distracting. Rudolph felt that any lionization of him would take energy away from the continuing fight for the well-being of the working reindeer. In a facile attempt to emulate their new hero, the other young reindeer began to wear bright red coverings on their noses. When Rudolph expressed his displeasure with this, some muttered that he was becoming too humorless and doctrinaire.

To Rudolph, this first agreement with Santa was to be just the beginning. He envisioned the eventual creation of a working reindeer's paradise, a toy-making and distribution collective where the means of production were shared by everyone. Unfortunately, many of the other reindeer began to take their newly won benefits as their inviolable right, bestowed by nature. They grew fat on too much moss and complained that their improved work schedules were still too taxing. Factions began to form among them about the best ways to invest their new pension fund. Rudolph tried to convince the dissident deer that they needed to stand united, but they began to resent his holier-than-thou attitude.

Some spread the rumor that he was an agent provocateur, sent by other aeronautically gifted animals seeking to gain Santa's favor and put the deer out of their jobs. While such theories were patently absurd, they served to discredit Rudolph and embolden his detractors. Eventually, he was voted out of the union he had helped establish. After this indignity, Rudolph decided to strike off for Lapland, where he felt the undomesticated reindeer were more in control of their own future.

And so, like other revolutionaries before him, Rudolph the angry young reindeer lived out the rest of his days in exile, bitterly wondering how a movement with such promise could prove to be so fragile in the end.

A CHRISTMAS CAROL

STAVE I—MARLEY'S POST-LIFE REPRESENTATIVE

arley was non-viable, to begin with; there is no doubt whatever about that, except for general philosophical questions about the permanence of death and the very real possibilities of reincarnation. The label "non-viable" is also fairly confining, yet, as Marley left no heirs or significant others, protests were not forthcoming. With his karma in the condition it was, chances were good that the host body that Marley's spirit might next inhabit would be of the invertebrate type, and until a champion for those speechless phyla comes forward, it is unlikely we shall ever hear from or about Marley again. So, for all practical purposes, Marley was as non-viable as a doornail. Unless you happen to be an animist, of course. But enough digression.

Scrooge certainly knew Marley had advanced into a post-life situation. The two had been business partners for many years, in a ruthless capitalistic operation that took advantage of people's caffeine addictions and exploited coffee farmers in developing nations. The business had started with good and generous intentions, and even offered stock options to the coffee farmers at one time, but these efforts had eroded over many years of competition and rapt attention to the bottom line. All that was left of their original egalitarian vision was a string of chrome-and-marble-filled coffee bars and a relaxed company dress code. While Marley was partly responsible for this reactionary shift, the real architect of this venal situation was his still-living partner.

Oh! But a tight-fisted hand at the grindstone was Scrooge! A squeezing, wrenching, grasping, scraping, clutching, covetous old sinner! And, as you might well imagine, this did nothing for his self-esteem. Oh, how long and wearisome life can be when hampered by a negative self-image!

Once upon a time—of all the good days in the year, on Christmas Eve (not to slight the importance of any day held holy by adherents of any other religion or non-religion, or of any other day not so designated)—Scrooge sat in his warehouse office, poring over the week's spreadsheets. It was cold, bleak, biting weather. The stock exchanges had only just closed, but outside it was quite dark already.

The door to Scrooge's office was kept open that he might keep an eye on his employees—of which there was now only one. The rest had been released just the previous week in the latest right-sizing of Scrooge & Marley, Inc. While these decruits had been released at an inauspicious time of year, Scrooge liked to think he had done them a favor by allowing them to pursue their own entrepreneurial interests. "Besides," thought he, "the taxes I've paid over the years have made unemployment benefits plenty attractive. These people are practically on Easy Street already."

Through the door Scrooge could see his lone administrative assistant, Roberto "Bob" Cratchit, busily inputting sales data. Poor Cratchit could almost see his breath, the temperature in the warehouse was kept so low. Scrooge led an ascetic lifestyle himself and expected others to do the same. He believed that excess heat and comfort sapped the human spirit and made the body susceptible to numerous diseases. And while his stated intents were to promote vitality and conserve fossil fuels, in his heart of hearts Scrooge more greatly relished the monetary savings of such an icy atmosphere. He kept the thermostat under lock and key in his office, so his staff of one was forced to make do with heavy coats, thick socks, and plenty of hot miso soup brought from home.

For you see, money was Scrooge's sole interest now, and only love. His life had not always been thus. As a youth, he was active in many progressive, humanitarian movements, mainly because he felt it was a good way to meet womyn. But he never in his life embraced himself as a worthwhile persun, and soon he began to distrust others as much as he distrusted himself. In his insecurity, he found comfort in accumulating wealth, since his money would never break his heart or ask to borrow his car. Such displaced affection would be merely sad in his isolated case, were it not so tragically prevalent in the world at large.

"A merry, non-sectarian Christmas, Uncle!" cried a cheerful voice. It was Scrooge's nephew, Fred, who had managed to sneak up on Scrooge and Cratchit.

"Bah!" said Scrooge. "Humbug!"

"Christmas a humbug, Uncle!" exclaimed Fred, whose cheerful face was quite ruddy from the cold. "You don't mean that, I am sure?"

"Yes," said Scrooge, "a humbug!" and swatted at his desk with a ledger. When he lifted the book, there sat the pasty remains of a rare Honduran humming cockroach.

"Uncle, how cruel!"

"We get these frequently with the bean shipments," replied Scrooge. "If I were to leave them alone, our interior environment would be overrun, so save your Rachel Carson act for someplace else. Now, what's all this hogwash about a merry Christmas? Mighty presumptuous of you."

"Then I amend it to 'Happy holidays.'"

"Still presumptuous."

"'Greetings of the season'?"

"Bah!" said Scrooge angrily. "I'm weary of this 'season' and all its forced gaiety. What is this season but the chance to feel another year older and not any more persunally fulfilled? A time to juggle the books for the end of the tax year? An opportunity to be

45

labelled unpatriotic if you don't splurge on enough baubles to buy your way into people's affections? If I could work my will, every idiot who spouts a 'Season's greetings' would be made to watch 'The Osmond Family Christmas Special' for a solid month and be force-fed 100 McDonald's eggnog shakes!"

"Uncle, you can't mean that."

"I can and do! And don't denigrate my opinions, Nephew! What good has this oppressive holiday ever done you?"

"Since you ask," replied Fred, "the holidays give me a chance to keep up appearances and assuage my middle-class guilt, so that I can drop a check in the mail and think I've done more than my share to better the world. It's a time when I'm told that everyone opens their hearts to the good in their fellow persuns, when rich and poor alike can drink in its kindness, delaying all-out class warfare for another year. So even if the holidays only reward me in trickle-down economic benefits and a warm fuzzy feeling, I should like to say I'm pretty much in favor of them, generally."

"Right on!" said Bob Cratchit.

"Enough from you!" Scrooge warned his staff.

"I'm surrounded by the cerebrally undercapitalized! What right have you to be merry? You're overextended enough."

"What right have you to be morose?" retorted his nephew. "Your catalog sales are big enough. I came to invite you over to our house tomorrow. My wife and I are having some people over, a little wine and cheese—strictly casual."

"Bah! I'd rather switch to decaf."

"We'll be playing Scattergories," coaxed his nephew.

"Good afternoon," said Scrooge.

"Then I'll just wish you enhanced seasonal benefits and a nurturing new year."

"Good afternoon!" said Scrooge.

His nephew left without an angry word, notwithstanding, and bestowed greetings of the season on Scrooge's assistant, who returned them gratefully.

Scrooge's phone rang, and he picked up the receiver to hear a chipper recorded voice say, "Happy holidays! . . . You have been selected to receive a wonderful free gift . . . of a lovely fruitcake and at the same time . . . help an organization working to better our community. To find out how to take advantage of this exciting offer . . . please remain on the line . . ."

Scrooge slammed down the receiver bitterly. "Humbug!" he muttered, and swatted another roach on his desk.

When five o'clock finally arrived, Roberto Cratchit cleared off his desk and prepared to leave. Scrooge strode over with a glowering look and said to his sole employee, "You'll want the entire day off tomorrow, I suppose?"

"We've been through this over and over," said Roberto. "If you really want someone here with you tomorrow, call a temp agency. If you want me here, you'll have to pay triple-time for the legal holiday, like my contract says."

Scrooge scoffed, "Bah! What could be 'legal' about picking a businessman's pocket in such a way? You just be careful to respect your body tomorrow and don't be hung over when you come in the day after."

Not in a mood to argue, Bob agreed to keep his excesses to a moderate level and left the warehouse. Scrooge stayed to work a few more hours, then turned off his lights and closed up. In the parking lot, he braced himself against the cold and climbed into his banged-up, well-traveled Volvo sedan. He could certainly have afforded a newer car, but the

Volvo's resale value had precipitously sunk and Scrooge wouldn't part with it for such a small figure. So determined was he to squeeze every last dime of value from the car that he didn't realize that the rear bumper was still attached only by the myriad bumper stickers that adorned it—bumper stickers for numerous worthy causes that were sadly stuck in mute testimony to the man's youthful idealism.

Scrooge soon reached his home, which stood at the far end of a nearly vacant condominium complex of renovated industrial buildings. He parked the Volvo near the main entrance and hurriedly opened the courtyard gate. Crossing the grim, unadorned cloister to his own door, he saw none of his neighbors, which suited him perfectly. Yet somehow he didn't feel alone.

He unlocked his front door, climbed the stairs, and entered his condo on the third floor. If this had ever been a welcoming domain, there was no trace of it now. The lights were kept perpetually dim, and to call the furnishings spartan would have been an insult to the inhabitants of that noble and ancient land. Scrooge thought that this sparseness imparted a certain air of Oriental spirituality to the place, but to a visitor (if Scrooge had ever had one) it merely looked cheap and underfurnished. From his entryway, he noticed that, for the first time in memory, the message light on his answering machine was blinking. Assuming it was another phone solicitation, he thought of ignoring it, yet the insistent red flashes caused him unease. With a hesitant motion, he pushed the playback button and heard what he thought was the voice of his terminally inconvenienced partner, Jacob Marley, in a mournful intonation. "Sssssscccrrooooooooggge!" * beep*

Scrooge slapped at the machine, annoyed by the seeming prank. "Bah!" he said, "I don't believe it!" and went into the kitchen. Recently he had read about the health benefits of a strict diet of watery gruel, and he had adopted this bleak and frugal regimen. He served up a bowl of the gruel (unheated, of course), took it into the living room, and settled into a cushion on the floor to eat. But no sooner had he done so than he heard an unearthly clattering in the courtyard. Scrooge stopped eating and listened. A sound arose like chains and heavy equipment being dragged over the trash cans. He made a mental note to talk to the condo board about extra security and double-bolted his door.

Scrooge jumped with a start at the next crash, which sounded like the door to his building being kicked in. He heard the clamor more loudly on the floors below, then coming up the stairs, then coming straight for his door.

"I still don't believe it," attested Scrooge.

But the blood drained from his face when the source of the noise pushed itself through his door. It was the post-life representative of Jacob Marley! The spirit was dressed in the jogging suit and expensive sneakers Marley favored in life, now worn and tattered from the grave. Around its head it wore a sweatband, but curiously under its chin rather than across its brow. The horrible clanking sounds Scrooge had heard came from a chain it carried that was fastened around its waist. The chain was made, Scrooge noticed, of barbells, abdominal exercisers, and random parts from broken Soloflex systems.

"Still working to feel the burn, eh, Jacob?" joked Scrooge uneasily.

"You don't believe in me?" asked the spectral visitor.

Scrooge said, "Usually I never question another's claims of spirituality, but I'm sorry, most people aren't so hammy about it." He tried to sound brave but wasn't very convincing.

"Why do you doubt your senses?" it asked.

"So now you're saying I should *believe* my senses?" asked a quick-thinking Scrooge, who often resorted to double-talk in sticky situations. "How limiting. Since when did Jacob Marley become a mere rationalist? Besides, if I were to believe my senses, it would look like I'm being haunted by the ghost of Jack La Lanne."

At this, the spirit raised a frightful cry and shook its chain with such a dismal and appalling noise that Scrooge clung tightly to his cushion in fear and fell over like a child's toy. But how much greater was the horror when the phantom removed the sweatband from around its head: Its jaw abruptly fell open and its teeth dropped out.

Scrooge got up on his knees, trembling. "Jacob, please," he begged. "Why have you come here? To show me false teeth?"

"That's just to start," said the non-corporeal visitor through its gums. "Do you know what else was false about me? Pectoral implants, calf implants, a hair weave, plastic surgery upon plastic surgery, even tinted contact lenses. Now in death I cannot tell which parts of me were original and which were paid for by installment. And because of this falsity, I am condemned to wander the world and witness those things which are genuine and true but in which I cannot share." Again the ghost let out a terrible cry. "I can never again visit southern California!"

Scrooge trembled and asked why he was fettered. "I wear the chain I forged in life," was the reply. "Each time I concentrated on the prefabricated and the superficial instead of the good and the true, I added another link to it. Do you realize the length of your own chain? It was this long seven years ago, and you have been working hard at it since."

"Have you no comfort to give me?" asked Scrooge.

"None. I know of your greed and your dual-visaged dealings. You value profits more than people, all in the name of some claptrap about the 'wisdom of the market' and 'a rising tide lifting all boats.' Such vanity! You know nothing about genuine worth, about what is truly valuable. Unless you mend your ways, you will receive a punishment worse than mine. My time here is nearly gone. I'm here to warn you that you still have a chance to escape my fate."

"You were always a good friend to me, Jacob," said Scrooge. "A good and dear friend, who knew me

POLITICALLY CORRECT HOLIDAY STORIES

better than I knew myself. May I take this opportunity to thank you for—"

"Enough of your sucking up!" the specter interrupted. "You can't talk your way out of this. You will be haunted this night by three extra-dimensional intercessors."

"Angels?" asked Scrooge brightly.

"Nothing so trendy. Expect the first when the clock strikes one."

"Can't I take them all at once," hinted Scrooge, "and get it over with?"

"They are individual spirits," answered Marley's shade, "each with different needs that must be respected. You'd do well to remember that." When it had said these words, the spirit picked up its teeth and bound its head again. It walked backward from Scrooge, and at every step Marley's post-life representative took, the window raised itself a little and was soon completely open. The spirit then floated out into the dark night with a mournful howl, and the window slammed fast.

Scrooge examined his door, which was still double-bolted. He tried to say "Humbug" but found himself vocally incapacitated. Whether it was the ordeal he had just experienced or the effect of the white-noise machine in the background, he crawled to his tatami mat in the bedroom and immediately fell asleep.

STAVE II—THE FIRST OF THE THREE SPIRITUAL FACILITATORS

t was still dark when Scrooge next awoke. Lying on his mat, he laughed to himself for what he believed had happened earlier. While he remained open to the possibility of extra-scientific phenomena, he couldn't validate the previous evening's event as anything credible. Marley's image had been so melodramatic, after all, not to mention self-righteous and accusatory. Additionally, an all-gruel diet was known to have some side effects, one of which was vivid hallucinations.

Just then the alarm on his wristwatch beeped once, and instantly a bright light pierced the darkness of his room. When his eyes adjusted, Scrooge saw before him a strange figure—a being not quite adult in stature, yet not quite child-like in appearance. Its hair, which was stylishly blown and brushed, was silver as if from experience, and yet the puckish face had not a wrinkle on it, as nearly as Scrooge could tell through its makeup. It wore a radiant sport coat with a boutonniere of holly. But the strangest thing about it was that from behind its head, there sprung a bright light—actually an entire bank of lights from the camera crew that it had brought along with it.

"Who and what are you?" demanded Scrooge, trying to sound brave.

"I am the Spirit whose coming was foretold to you," it said into its microphone. "I am the Ghost of Christmas Retrospective, and this is my crew."

Scrooge asked the Spirit why it had brought all the cameras.

The Spirit said, "Nobody is really afraid of ghosts anymore. They all think I'm some sort of hologram or special effect. But come in with a hard-bitten, exposé-hungry camera crew, and you get people's attention."

"And what is it you want from me?"

"There are allegations that your life has been spent worshiping false idols and turning your back on the rest of persunkind. Would you care to comment on that?" The Spirit stuck its microphone in Scrooge's face.

He smiled smugly. "You must really take me for someone of overtaxed mental and emotional resources. I don't respond to anonymous allegations."

"Then you are telling us that you are the model of a concerned, conscientious, upright citizen?"

"Yes," Scrooge asserted, and added another untruth, "although definitely not wedded to the established order of things."

"Then we must have been mistaken," said the Spirit with a straight face. "I smell another story here. What do you say we review with you some of the events that shaped the upstanding man you are today?"

Scrooge saw nothing wrong with this and readily agreed. The Spirit had him sign a release then led him over to the window. "Wait a minute," said Scrooge. "We're three floors up. I'll fall."

"Give but a touch to my microphone cord," said the Spirit, "and you'll be borne aloft. But strap on this safety helmet anyway; I don't need any more lawsuits. And . . . we're rolling."

As these words were spoken, Scrooge, the Spirit, and the camera crew passed through the wall and suddenly found themselves in the midst of bedlam. A horde of people in gaudy and disheveled clothing surged and careened around them, while disco music pulsed loudly and incessantly. Amid laughter and occasional howling, men and womyn were telling persunal secrets, hidden desires, and undecorous jokes with an incredible amount of informality. But it apparently was all in excellent fun, at least by that era's standards. In this elegant, crowded hotel ballroom, the holiday cheer spilled as much from the hearts of the celebrants as out of the numerous glasses held aloft.

"And where are we now?" the Spirit asked as he shoved the mike in Scrooge's face.

Scrooge yelled over the din, "My gosh! This is one of the office parties that old Fezziwig used to throw, before the feds got him. It's good to see it all again—it was so hard to remember the morning after."

Scrooge recognized many old friends and acquaintances amidst the faces assembled there. He shouted out their names in recognition, but they paid him no mind, as was their prerogative as shades of the past. These slights worried Scrooge not a bit as he was swept up in a wave of nostalgia and festivity. He quite forgot himself amid all the merry-making and tried to join a "Soul Train" line. The Spirit and its crew watched bemusedly, feeling no obligation to stop him from his frivolity. The release they'd made him sign clearly stated that these were merely images of the past that would not be aware of his presence.

As the shades continued to eat, drink, and cele-brate each others' company, the Spirit asked point-edly, "In your opinion, was Fezziwig misusing corporate assets, as the indictments charged?"

"Misusing? Not at all!" replied Scrooge. "Fezziwig was a great man, and a wonderful employer."

"But he allegedly funneled corporate assets into a secret budget to pay for a lavish persunal lifestyle, which included throwing these wild parties."

"Everyone looked forward to these parties. They were the highlight of the year. They were wonderful for morale."

"But they must have cost so much."

"For how happy he made us, whatever he paid was an absolute bargain."

"Then we can assume that you've adopted Fezziwig's philosophy and throw extravagant parties for your own employees?" the Spirit said into its microphone.

Scrooge paused a minute. "We prefer to invest in our company's human capital in other ways. We give our employees the chance to pursue whatever is meaningful for them in the celebration sector."

The Spirit asked, "Is that why you only coughed up for a coupon book for Cratchit this year?" Scrooge's face turned red from embarrassment as he stammered, "No comment." He thought to himself that maybe he did owe a little more to the memory of his mentor Fezziwig.

The Spirit pointed to a dark corner of the ballroom and said, "In addition to food and music, it appears the opportunities were endless for sexual harassment as well." He and his crew rushed over, lights blazing, while Scrooge followed in the rear. In that dark corner were a man and a wommon, locked in passionate embrace. Scrooge found it fairly amusing until the couple paused for a breath of air. "Candy!" he shouted.

In an instant the ballroom had disappeared, and Scrooge, the Spirit, and the crew found themselves standing in the back of a dark restaurant. At the table in front of them sat a younger image of Scrooge, as well as the wommon with whom this younger man had just been entwined at the party.

"I thought it would be fun, is all, marrying you," she was saying. "But I was a lot younger five months ago. Emotionally, anyway."

The Spirit asked, "And who's this we're watching?"

"Candy," said Scrooge. "She was my second wife."

The wommon continued. "I never would have gone through with it, had I known you were so divorced from your feelings. You keep me and everyone else at arm's length, then try to double-talk your way out of any real connection."

"Candy, I won't say you're wrong," said the younger Scrooge. "But how many people know themselves well enough to realize that they *are* divorced from their feelings? If I were to admit it, I might even consider this insight a kind of progress."

"Oh!" said Candy incredulously. "Oh! Oh, sure! Oh!"

Suddenly Candy disappeared, and in her place sat another young wommon. "Besides which," this wommon said, "you ought to know I'm not the type of wife who'll smile bravely while her husband holds press conferences to try and clear his name."

"Ahhh!" screamed the genuine Scrooge.

"And who would this be?" asked the Spirit.

"That's Sandy," he replied. "She was my third wife."

"I don't know what you're talking about," said Scrooge's younger image.

"Yeah, right," she said, rather ungraciously. "I know all about the stock split and how you're going to screw those poor coffee farmers."

The younger Scrooge slapped the table. "We're totally within the law on that one!"

"I don't care," she said coolly. "I'm leaving. It's not pleasant watching you sell off your ideals one by one." Then, in an instant, she was gone also, replaced by yet another wommon. The real Scrooge said, without being prompted, "That's Brandy, my fourth wife."

"Fourth?" asked the Spirit. "Guess again."

Scrooge looked panicked. "Fifth?" he asked, not at all sure whether he was correct. And as he stood there watching another set of the angry good-byes at the table, Scrooge's unbelieving eyes were treated to a parade of the womyn in his life. Ex-wives, paramours, common-law wives, sexual surrogates— he got some names wrong, as well as their order of appearance in his life; but they all had the same thing to tell his younger self: He was distant and cold, he worshipped success at the expense of his own integrity, he had used each one for his own selfish purposes, and he would be hearing from their lawyers the next day.

"Spirit, take me home," implored Scrooge. "I can bear this no longer. I can't even keep their names straight."

"But we have more scenes to visit," said the Spirit, "and we have plenty of tape left. What about this union crew? Do you know what this is costing me?"

"No! Take me home! This interview's over!" Scrooge leapt at the camera that had been in his face and tried to grab it from its operator. The Spirit and the rest of the crew wrestled Scrooge away from the equipment, and the melee continued until Scrooge awoke, alone in his bedroom, doing battle with a floor cushion. Sweating and panting heavily, he went to the bathroom, swallowed a couple of Nytol, then staggered back to his mat and immediately fell asleep.

crooge next awoke when his watch buzzed the hour. He peered around but saw no spirits to pester him. Yet an eerie light suffused his bed chamber and intimated that he might not be alone. The source of this light seemed to be in his living room, so Scrooge rose from his mat and walked to the door. He opened the door with his breath held fast and peeked in.

What he saw astounded him. Instead of the usual postmodern grays and whites, the room seemed almost on fire with a profusion of warm, yellow light from the Yule log blazing in the hearth. The walls and ceiling were so richly festooned with garlands of holly, mistletoe, evergreen, and ivy that it was as if a rain forest in all its biodiversity had been transplanted there. Heaped up on the floor, to form a type of throne, were geese, game, brawn, great joints of meat, suckling pigs, long strings of sausages, mince pies, plum puddings, barrels of oysters, immense cakes, and steaming bowls of punch—all with enough empty calories and cholesterol to clog the veins of an entire peacekeeping force. At the sight of such an amount of food, the normally temperate Scrooge nearly swooned, half from raven-ousness and half from revulsion. In easy state upon this throne sat a jolly figure of greater-than-average stature, glorious to see, who bore in his hand a glowing torch, which he raised up high to shed light on Scrooge as he came peeping round the door.

"Come in!" exclaimed the Spirit. "Come in and know me better."

Scrooge approached timidly, and asked him not to wave the torch so near to the sprinklers in his ceiling. "Oh, lighten up a little," laughed the visitor. "Look upon me! I am the Ghost of Christmas Present. Let's party!"

Scrooge raised his eyes as he was told. He was relieved to see the warm and jovial look in the Spirit's bearded face. This specter would apparently be less confrontational and insinuating than the last. The Spirit was clothed in a simple yet generously cut green robe that hung loosely on his abundant frame. His dark brown curls were long and free, as free as his unconstrained demeanor and joyful air. Then Scrooge noticed, standing behind the Spirit, another figure, who was more slight and sober in aspect than the other, though not unpleasant. "Who is your companion?" Scrooge asked.

"Oh, him? He's Rupert, my designated driver. Can you believe it? Ha!" The Spirit rose and said, "C'mon, touch my robe. Let's blow this taco stand!" Scrooge did as he was told, and the room and everything in it vanished instantly.

The next moment, they stood in the humble dwelling of a family that existed in a lower percentile of socioeconomic strata. Despite their situation, the family members refused to play the victim, and were chipper and merry in the delights of the season. Love and respect decorated their home as wonderfully as their flocked arboreal companion. The aromas of their dinner lingered welcomingly as the family sat together on the couch, watching *It's a Wonderful Life* on their flickering television. The

Spirit inspected the scene fondly yet intently, then whistled at Rupert and jerked his thumb backward over his shoulder.

Before Scrooge could blink his eyes, he and his companions were transported to a more opulent residence, owned by members of the oppressing class. People were gathered there for an intimate soiree, where they traded confidential and exclusionary information that further secured their privileged positions in society. Food and wine were laid out in abundance, and the guests feasted with little regard for the needs of the workers they exploited. But class warfare was far from their minds this night. The men and womyn were in grand high spirits as they sat around the entertainment center together, watching a laser disc recording of *It's a Wonderful Life*.

Scrooge was struck by the genuine warmth the people displayed for one another while still respecting each other's persunal space. He had not felt such warmth for years, and at this moment was acutely aware of its absence. "Spirit, why do you show me these images?" he finally asked. "Are you trying to show me how isolated I am from my fellow human persuns? How much I have sealed up my heart from the rest of the world? How love is the common link for us all?"

"Nah," said the Spirit from the buffet table a short distance away, "we're just here to raid the 'fridge." He walked back to Scrooge, munching on a large sandwich he had thrown together. The Spirit motioned to the TV. "Y'know, I walk in on people watching this movie just about all night, and I *still* have never seen the ending. Can you believe it? Ha! Let's make like a baby and head out!"

And in the briefest of intervals, the three astral travelers landed in an apartment in the city. It was sparsely furnished yet tidy, and the television had been turned off ("Thank a non-sectarian heaven," thought Scrooge). He could hear voices, a man's and a wommon's, one of which was particularly familiar.

"I don't know," the wommon said, "things just don't feel festive enough to me."

"Do you want to pop the 'Fireplace Log' video in the VCR again?" asked the man.

"Bob Cratchit!" Scrooge blurted out. "Is this his house? And is this Mercedes, the persun with whom he has a primary relationship? My word!"

The Cratchits continued their conversation, unaware of the presence of Scrooge or the Spirits. Mercedes sighed, "No, but it just doesn't feel as joyful and exciting these days as when I was a little girl. There are times when I wish I could stop being an atheist, if only for a little while. If only there were more holidays on the calendar for the deistically unencumbered."

From the kitchen came the loud crash of a platter hitting the floor. Scrooge looked in the direction of the noise and saw the big-boned Spirit of Christmas Present emerge, carrying a turkey leg and wearing a comically innocent expression. Roberto ran into the kitchen to investigate. "It must have been the dog," the Spirit suggested, rather speciesistically, as he toddled across the room.

"It must have been the dog," echoed Roberto, who picked up the mess and put the food in the refrigerator.

Scrooge eyed the corpulent spirit with an unmasked disgust. "If you don't have any respect for yourself," he sniffed, "at least try to have some for others."

"Aw, lighten up, man, it's Christmas Eve!" said the Spirit as he alternated bites of turkey leg with fistfuls of Chex party mix. "And the bigger I am, the more of me there is to love. Ha!"

As Roberto walked back into the room, Mercedes said to him, "I think I'm also depressed about how little money is coming in."

"Now, Mercedes," said Roberto comfortingly, "don't fall into the trap of our materialistic culture. We have a roof over our heads, enough food, good friends, a loving child . . ."

"Oh, Roberto, don't talk to me about traps. You're obviously ensnared in a ridiculous 'nobility in poverty' concept that the bourgeois class generates to appease its own guilt. We're not virtuous paupers languishing in some Dickens novel. We've got bills to pay, and that ogre Scrooge refuses to pay you a fair wage."

"I'm trying my best to wreak anarchy at the office," explained Roberto. "I'm striking back at Scrooge in his pocketbook by stealing photocopies and taking too long on coffee breaks. He and the heartless system he represents will come tumbling down before too long." Scrooge was taken aback. He had no idea that Roberto was so bitter, but then again, he rarely talked with his employee about anything in a frank way, and he knew almost nothing of his family life.

"But how does that help us?" asked Mercedes. "How does that help Diminutive Timón? With that huge deductible required by Scrooge's miserable insurance coverage, we'll never be able to afford proper medical care for him."

As if on cue, their vertically challenged pre-adult came into the room. Diminutive Timón was an amiable chap and full of boundless energy. In fact, the only trait that would set him apart from the others in his gender peer group was that his size did not conform to the average. He jumped onto the couch and hugged his caregivers, whose concerns melted away, if only momentarily.

Scrooge's heart was touched by the little pre-adult. He turned and asked, "This boy, Diminutive Timón, what is the matter with him?"

"Nobody knows," Rupert said. "His repeated willfulness and bursts of uncontrollable energy have everyone perplexed. At first it was thought his behavior was a simple case of blocked chakras. But now his condition appears to be a birth-induced delayed trauma disorder."

Scrooge was appalled. "Are there no specialists? Are there no telethons for victims such as he?"

"Don't call him a victim," Rupert said, "he's merely a persun living with a disorder. And telethons, well, they're a little infantilizing, you'd have to admit."

Scrooge thought for a moment, then asked, "Spirit, is his outlook so irretrievably bleak?"

The Spirit of Christmas Present looked him in the face, although his eyes were getting glassy. With bits of food dangling from his beard, he said, "If you'd spring for better coverage, you tightwad, at least they could pay for more tests and treatments."

Properly chastened, Scrooge watched the family play together. How nondysfunctional they were, even with Timón's affliction. Scrooge sadly envied their warmth and their positive, nurturing interaction. After a while Bob announced it was time to toast the season. He got out the glasses and the sparkling mineral water and passed them out to Mercedes and Timón. "A toast," he said, "to this festive season, and may the forces that placed us here (or not) continue to bless us."

Timón raised his glass. "May a higher entity (if there is such a thing) bless us, every one."

They sipped in unison. Then Roberto raised his glass and said, "To Mr. Scrooge . . ."

Mercedes stopped and set down her glass. "Really, Roberto, why spoil our celebration by mentioning him?"

"You didn't let me finish," said Roberto. "To Mr. Scrooge, for so perfectly embodying the enemy of the working class. May he always inspire us to continue the fight!"

Mercedes laughed, and so did Timón. They all raised their glasses and drank. And their laughter and joy continued until the Spirit slurringly announced it was time to move on. As the scene faded, Scrooge continued to stare, and especially kept his eye on Diminutive Timón.

The next sound Scrooge heard (besides the fairly regular moaning of the Spirit of Christmas Present) was the hearty laughter of his nephew. Soon Fred's cozy living room materialized around them, with all his guests who had come there to feast.

"And so Uncle Scrooge just sat there," continued his nephew, "refusing to accept any of my good wishes for the season and swatting away at the bugs on his desk!"

Everyone laughed heartily when picturing the kindness-impaired coffee distributor in such a scene. Until, that is, one persun in the group said icily, "I don't think cruelty to defenseless insects is all that funny."

Fred's countenance changed to a concerned expression. "No, you're right, I'm sorry," he murmured.

The Spirit guffawed and said something disparaging about the group's sexual adequacy, which they

74

were lucky they couldn't hear. In fact, the Spirit laughed so hard at his remark that he lost his balance and stumbled over a footstool with a heavy thump. Scrooge was by now supremely annoyed at the Spirit's loutish behavior. "What's the deal with him?" he asked Rupert finally. "I haven't seen him drink anything."

"It's a substance abuse problem," said the driver. "He thrives on the milk of human kindness, but sometimes he enjoys too much of it."

"You got that right, Rupert buddy," slurred the Spirit as he pulled himself unsteadily to his feet. "And you know the old saying: You can't drink the milk of human kindness; you can only rent it. Excuse me a minute." The Spirit staggered off, looking for relief.

The mood of the celebrants picked up again when Fred's wife announced, "You'll all be happy to know that we managed to dissuade all the local retailers from carrying mistletoe this year. So let's drink a toast to the end of traditionally sanctioned sexual harassment."

They all raised their glasses of non-alcoholic, low-fat, no-cholesterol eggnog, all except one. "Sasha?" Fred asked of this persun. "Is something wrong with the eggnog?"

"You've forgotten," said Sasha quietly. "I'm a vegan."

Fred's face went red. He mumbled numerous apologies and ran into the kitchen to prepare Sasha a beet-juice spritzer. This slight error did not dampen people's spirits long, however, and the festiveness and generosity of the season soon returned. Good cheer and laughter filled the air at the expense of no individual persun or group.

Scrooge got quite caught up in the merrymaking and clapped and cheered gaily at the games and jests the celebrants enjoyed. Fred's guests played at Optically Inconvenienced Persun's Bluff for a good long time, then enjoyed a lively round of Twenty Non-Intrusive Questions. Next they worked at decorating their Yule tree in the most inclusive and equitable way imaginable. Oh! what fun they had, adorning it with Stars of David and menorahs, and oriental dragons and Shinto paper cranes, and stars and crescent moons, and dream catchers of all sizes. They hung holly clusters for the druids, talismans for the Wiccans, and yin-yangs, ankhs, I Ching sticks, Tarot cards, rune stones, and all conceivable manner of symbols and mandalas. When they were finished, the tree stood gloriously and ecumenically arrayed.

Next on the agenda were refreshments, and Fred's guests did eat well. They feasted on salads and casseroles, fruits and nuts, and naturally sweetened pies and cookies until they could find no more room inside themselves. To Scrooge's vexation, the Spirit of Christmas Present could not help remarking disdainfully on the fare, which was too healthful and delicate for his tastes. While he pounded his fists and bellowed that he was starving, the guests heard not a word. Scrooge and the designated driver both noticed how the strong currents of goodwill were causing the Spirit to act very erratically. After the Spirit began to flail about and knocked a platter of baba ganoush on himself, Rupert led him out to the patio where the fresh air would clear his head.

To top off the feast, Fred brought out from the kitchen a steaming platter of low-fat latkes, with generous bowls of apple sauce and yogurt. Although everyone was full to bursting, they couldn't resist gobbling a few of the potato pancakes. As the guests settled down around the living room, Fred brought out a menorah he had purchased just that day and placed a candle in each of the eight holes. He recited what he knew about the Festival of Lights (which admittedly was very little) and lit all eight candles, thus compressing a salute to Hanukkah to fit into their busy evening.

Next Fred brought out a straw mat and placed it under the menorah. "Now it's time for our Kwanzaa celebration," he announced. "You'll please forgive me for using the menorah again, but I didn't have time to find a proper *kinara* at the store." So the guests quickly honored the *Nguzo Saba*, or Seven Principles, while Fred led them in song and mangled the Swahili words he read from his Kwanzaa manual. They then cleared the table for their celebration of Divali, for their guests of the Hindu persuasion. By the time the overstuffed piñatas were brought out for the next phase of the party, Scrooge had walked out to the patio to look for his two astral guides. Out in the cold December air, he spied the Spirit of Christmas Present flat on his back, making hooting noises and laughing at his own private jokes.

"So, where are we off to next?" asked Scrooge.

"Our time with you is almost at an end," Rupert said. "After the Spirit gets this full of the milk of human kindness, any further travel tends to be counterproductive, not to mention embarrassing." The Spirit had begun singing "Deck the Halls" loudly, substituting "Fa La La" for all the lyrics he was forgetting (practically all of them, it turned out).

Scrooge asked hopefully, "Then is my reeducation over? Have I not been visited by three spirits tonight?"

Rupert said, "I'm not really a spirit of the season, just a concerned observer. You still have one more spirit to meet." Rupert took the hands of the prostrate Spirit and began to drag him away. As they left, the scene changed, and Scrooge found himself standing in the middle of a cold and lonely plain, with another specter of gloomy visage walking toward him out of the murk.

STAVE IV: THE LAST (BUT IN NO WAY LEAST) OF THE SPIRITUAL FACILITATORS

he phantom slowly, gravely, silently approached. When it came near him, Scrooge bent down upon his knee, for in the very air through which this Spirit moved, the wraith seemed to scatter gloom and mystery. For which, of course, we can only blame our own fears and insecurities, which we habitually project onto the unknown.

The Spirit was dressed all in black—scuffed black boots, black leather jacket, baggy black shorts, torn black stockings—with an occasional glint from the studs, chains, hoops, and buckles that adorned the specter's clothing and various bodily parts. Beneath a haystack of bleached and ratted hair, a gaunt, expressionless face was visible, highlighted garishly in mascara and black lipstick. As the Spirit shambled slowly and somewhat absently toward him, Scrooge could not make out the phantom's gender (not that such an unimportant variable would be any reflection on his/her skills or authority). When s/he stepped beside Scrooge, his/her mysterious presence and the smell of tobacco and stale beer filled the man with a solemn dread.

"I am in the presence of the Ghost of Christmas Yet to Come?" said Scrooge.

The Spirit answered not, but coughed, scratched, and pointed onward with a hand.

"You are about to show me shadows of the things that will happen in the time before us," pursued Scrooge. "Is that so, Spirit?"

The Spirit looked at him without emotion, then gave him the quick combination of a shrug, a nod, and a sneer, which Scrooge took to mean assent.

"Ghost of the Future!" he exclaimed. "I fear you more than any other, because I'm a bit of a control freak and dread the idea of looking into the unknown. I felt that I was making real progress with the last Spirit before he became incoherent. Some real growth was happening there. But I know your purpose is to instruct me in the truth, so I place myself in your hands. Lead on."

They walked, but made no apparent progress along the misty ground. Instead, the city seemed to spring up around them and encompass them of its own act. The buildings and byways were familiar to Scrooge immediately. Up ahead in the cold street were a man and a wommon, whom Scrooge recognized as reporters to whom he had often leaked damaging stories about his competitors and other enemies.

"I don't know what he died of," said the first reporter. "All I know is, he's dead."

"It must have been a stake through the heart," joked her companion, "that is, if they could find his heart."

The first reporter sighed, emitting an icy cloud. "He's causing me grief even in the grave. He couldn't have picked a worse time to die. It throws a wrench into the exposé I was wrapping up on his Central American land-holdings. Now I won't be able to confront him with anything on camera."

"Talk to some of the organizers of the farmers' revolt down there," suggested her companion. "You'll get some good video. They're probably dancing in the streets right now."

The reporters laughed at that idea and walked on. Scrooge turned to the Spirit and asked, "Who did they mean, Spirit? What man were they talking about?" The phantom made no reply, but coughed and pointed onward. Scrooge's figure trembled from head to foot as he thought of his nephew's warm, friendly living room. "I'll tell you this at the outset," he informed the Spirit, "I'm not very good with this whole death concept."

Farther down the street, Scrooge and his malnourished guide walked up on two men emerging from an office, putting on their overcoats and fastening their scarves against the cold. From the section of town, one could assume their profession most likely was the law. One man told the other, "Without a will, eh? That's going to be some catfight."

"It'll be years in probate," was the reply. "The creditors are one thing, but with an estate that size, those ex-wives will not give up easily."

"They should watch what they ask for," replied the first. "Any stake in that little empire is going to be worth a lot less, once the legal fees come due."

"Well, look at it this way," chortled the second, "he might have avoided paying for our services while alive, but our fair share of his money was bound to come due eventually!" The laughing barristers proceeded down the street, their steps growing ever lighter as they contemplated the great bounty of billable hours.

Scrooge was shaken by their callousness. "I hate to watch a legal mind busy at its ravening work," he told the Spirit. "Parasites, one and all. I might have ruined a few companies and careers in my time, but I never charged a fee for it or pretended I was providing a service."

Because of what he knew of the Spirit's mission, Scrooge tried to find a lesson for himself in all he was witnessing, but the scenes only filled him with dread and revulsion. The relentless silence of the ghostly visitor did not help to soothe him. "Who was this dead man?" he asked. "Is there nothing but cynicism and avarice attached to his demise? Can you not show me something constructive that came of this lost life, or someone for whom his presence and his passing have mattered?"

The Spirit looked at him solemnly, then gave him the same quick shrug-nod-sneer as before. S/he pointed around a corner, and Scrooge proceeded as indicated through the chilly murk. Turning the bend, they found themselves in a wholly new part of town, heading toward a nondescript building whose outsize dimensions were well illumined with spot-lights. Scrooge and his spiritual facilitator drifted past a crowd of patient, shivering people in a line outside the building and melted their way through the cement walls. When they emerged on the other side, they found themselves in the wings of a television studio filled with a live audience. Scrooge recognized it as the set of one of those daytime tabloid talk shows that exploited cheap titillation and personal failures for prodigious ratings. The moderator of the show roamed the audience with a microphone, while her guest for the broadcast sat in a chair onstage.

"And can you share with us what happened after that?" asked the moderator.

"Well, the lack of money in the house always caused tension between my parents," explained the guest, "and all their concerns about my health added to the bad atmosphere there. It was years before my correct diagnosis was revealed, and by that time so much damage had been done to my family that it almost fell apart."

"And tell us, what was your diagnosis?"

"I have acute psycho-environmental allergies," he said bravely, "which means that all the people, all the places, all the objects that make up my surroundings can without warning make my anxiety level go sky-high, and at times give me severe headaches and even a mild rash."

"And you blame your father's employer for all this?"

"Yes, he worked my father to the bone, and provided such shabby health coverage that I went improperly diagnosed for many years."

The host asked, "What was your reaction to the recent news of that man's death?"

The guest sighed. "Relief. I felt justice had been served. Then I felt incredible guilt and anger for my feelings of relief. This man had somehow wormed his way into my mind and wouldn't let go. For all the damage he'd done to me in his life, it still hadn't relented when he was gone. That's why I wrote my book: to purge myself of his influence and make friends with myself again."

"All right, we have to take a break," said the host. "The book is called *My Oppressor, Myself.* We'll be back for more with Timón Cratchit, right after this."

The audience burst into applause on cue, the sound of which caused Scrooge to jump. He stared incredulously at the man on the stage. He certainly looked like Bob Cratchit's son, although no longer diminutive at all. To Scrooge, he looked hale and hearty, in spite of his pious and pitiable expression.

"What is this all about?" he demanded of the Spirit. "How could Timón's fate be tied to mine? I'd never seen him before last night and I expressed enough concern then, even though he merely looked like a regular, rambunctious boy to me. I thought you were here to see to *my* welfare. Why have you shown me this? What am I to do with his whiny revelation?" The Spirit looked at him puzzledly, as if a bit nonplussed at this reaction. It appeared that getting the message through to this mortal would be a bigger challenge than anticipated. The specter paused, apparently weighing its next move, then pointed onward as s/he had so often before.

They passed through the wall of the studio and were suddenly at the gates of a cemetery, where the snow whistled through the twisty weeds that choked the unkept grounds. The Spirit stood among the graves, coughing and pointing down to one headstone. Scrooge was disoriented and shivering. His pulse began to race as he sensed his journey with the phantom was drawing to a disturbing close.

"Why have we come here?" he asked. "I've already told you, I don't deal with these kinds of things well."

The Spirit again pointed at the stone, beckoning the man to read it. "I know intellectually that this is all part of the great cycle of life," Scrooge explained, "but I have a real problem with it emotionally. And you, Spirit, have become a very depressing companion. All these cheap theatrics aren't doing me much good at all. Ask of me anything else, but please don't make me read the stone."

The Spirit was immoveable as ever. Scrooge crept forward, trembling as he went. He pushed aside the weeds and read the stone of the neglected grave, upon which was carved his own name, EBENEZER SCROOGE.

"No, Spirit, no!" he cried. "Now you've gone too far. The other spirits worked my emotions over well enough. Now you come along to intimidate me with all these scenarios and alleged conversations, only to bring me here to confront me with my own mortality! I've never heard of such flagrant entrapment!"

Scrooge angrily dusted the snow from his hands and began to rise to his feet. "You and your pals ought to look at yourselves in the mirror before coming around to improve other people's characters. All this manipulation, all this sordid play-acting! On top of all the insults and indignities that have been heaped on me tonight, you decide to show me that I may die! Well, forget it! Enough is enough! I reject it, and I reject you!"

The Spirit's eyes were wide with amazement. This was indeed a first in his/her sepulchral experience: a man confronted with his own inevitable demise, who attests that for himself it is merely an option.

"Take me back to that TV show," said Scrooge, "and I'll show that little crybaby Timón something. I'll show him the pressures of owning a business and employing subversive ingrates like his father." Scrooge approached the Spirit menacingly. The Spirit, eyes wide and darting back and forth, took a few steps in retreat. "Take me back to those reporters and I'll show them what bunch of leeches and lemmings they are. They want to confront me on camera—I'll give 'em some good video."

Scrooge now had the Spirit's arm and was holding fast, while the phantom, at a total loss, began struggling to get away. "Take me to them all! I'll tell that bunch of whiners where to get off! They expect the business owner to have all the answers and solve all their problems, then they despise him for their own helplessness! They don't know what I go through! I deserve better treatment than this!"

And as they wrestled, Scrooge saw the Spirit go through a transformation. The hair shrank, the body went limp, and Scrooge found himself wrestling with an oversize arrangement of dried flowers.

STAVE V:
THE END OF EVERYTHING

es! And the dried flower arrangement was his own. The sleeping mat was his own, the halogen lamp was his own. Best of all, the time before him was his own, to plan his revenge in!

"It's over! I am done!" said Scrooge in relief. "The Spirits have finished their work, all in one night! And Jacob Marley, take heed: They did not beat me!"

Scrooge sprang from his mat and paced the room, inspecting everything there to make certain he was awake. All the while, he continued to talk to himself: "What nerve, rubbing images of possible mortality in my face. They *all* had their nerve, trying to make me feel guilty! Ha! If anything, they showed me that I'm the product of my environment! All the pressures put on white males! It's no wonder I am the way I am! It's not my fault at all!"

He charged out into the living room, not even pausing to put his clothes on properly. He was too excited, too indignant, too ready to act on what the Spirits had shown him. "Thanks, Jacob! You sent the ghosts here, that I might discover what's real and true! And I found out the truth about what I'd imagined all along: Everyone's against me and blames me for their problems. So who's the real victim here? Me! That's who!"

These revelations sent Scrooge into giddy fits. He made many plans for his day, and for the near future. "I'll start a radio show to address the abused and underappreciated white males in this country," he said to the empty room. "No, a cable network. No, better still—I'll run for office, to protect the interests of white males and businessmen everywhere! Whoop! Ha ha!" And Scrooge laughed at himself and his agitation, a laugh that would certainly chill anyone who heard it.

Without even pausing for his usual gruel-pancake breakfast, Scrooge left his condo hurriedly—there was so much he had to do! He had to fire Bob Cratchit for his pilfering and sponging! He had to draw up a will, and leave each of his ex-wives a big goose egg! He had so many things to do, but first he had to get to his office. Where was his Volvo?

"Ah me, I'm so giddy and excited, I must have walked right past it! Ha ha!" Scrooge retraced his steps in the small parking lot then spun round again. He knew exactly where he'd parked it the night before, but now that space was utterly vacant. "What! Where?" screamed an incredulous Scrooge. "Where is it? Who'd want to steal a nineteen-year-old Volvo?!"

Infuriated, he was about to storm back inside to phone the police when yet another bright light flashed before him and left him visually nonreceptive for the moment. When he recovered, he saw in front of him what must have been another spirit, yet the appearance of this one was the most mundane and ordinary of any he had seen (not that there isn't some magick to be found in the mundane and ordinary).

There before him stood what appeared to be a middle-aged wommon in a navy-blue polyester suit that lagged severely behind the fashion curve. She wore her hair up in a pile that was slightly askew, and her glasses were perched at the end of her nose and fixed around her neck on a chain. In her hand was a metal clipboard, which she perused. She had about her an air of complete indifference. On the lapel of her jacket she wore a plastic pin to celebrate the season, a cute Saint Nicholas that moved like a jumping jack (or jill) when its little string was pulled.

"Mr. Scrooge?" she asked, without looking up from her clipboard. "Ebenezer Scrooge?"

"That is I," he said, somewhat testily. "What do you want of me? I'm in a terrible rush."

"I'm sure you are," she said emotionlessly. She flipped a few pages, then looked up. "I'm here to offer an official apology for all that happened last night. It was something of a mix-up."

Scrooge couldn't believe his ears. "What? Who are you? How do you know of last night?"

"I am the Supervisory Spirit of Intercessory Therapeutics," the specter said. "I'm in charge of coordinating the caseload of all the spiritual facilitators that are working to help persuns change for the better at this time of year. I sent the Spirits to you last night, as well as Rupert the driver. But my orders were somewhat garbled when I received them, and I'm afraid you were subjected to the wrong therapy last night."

Scrooge's mouth hung open. Even with everything he'd been through, such a thunderbolt he never expected! He felt his anger begin to rise. "What do you mean, 'wrong therapy'? How could such a thing be?"

"We do our best, but mistakes do happen."

"What about Marley? He—"

"It's no use blaming any particular shade. You must understand, we reeducate thousands of persons every day, and we're especially busy at this time of year. You yourself must realize how hard it is to get work done during the holidays."

"Meddling, incompetent spiritual bureaucracies!" groused Scrooge.

"I apologize for any inconvenience," the Supervisor said, officiously and insincerely, "but this is for your own good and everyone else's. According to your psychological profile, Mr. Scrooge, last night's method of therapy would be of no help to you, and might even reinforce your negative traits. I'm afraid this may have already happened. However, there are other treatments."

"What other treatments?" demanded Scrooge. "I'll not allow—"

"There is Past Regression–Future Progression, which you had last night. For the severely despondent, we have Negative Alternative Outcome treatment, which we in the profession refer to as a 'George Bailey' session. But for you, Mr. Scrooge, we have something much more direct and traumatic. But it is for your own good, trust me."

"What do you mean, 'traumatic'?" he asked. "Last night was no walk in the park."

"Your treatment plan calls for Rapid Materialistic Voidance," the Supervisor explained. "In it, you will be deprived of all the worldly attachments on which you place so much importance. In order to improve your character, we are forced to ruin your business. To start with, a government report is going to be released tomorrow, showing a definitive link between coffee drinking and liver disease. The price of your stock will plummet, and all your stockholders, including yourself, will take a tremendous loss."

Scrooge looked panicked. "No! Wait a moment! I have to get to my warehouse!"

"You needn't bother. It's already in flames and quite beyond salvage."

This second blow sent Scrooge reeling. The work of a lifetime, up in flames—and he'd decided to let his insurance lapse just last week! "This is too much," he said in a shaky voice. "I need a drink of water. Let me go inside a minute."

"Oh, I almost forgot," the Supervisor said. From her pocket she took a small remote-control box, fumbled to turn it the proper side up, then punched a large red button with her thumb. Heavens, the ear-splitting sound! A fierce, fiery explosion blew out the windows of Scrooge's apartment, scattering debris and broken glass throughout the courtyard. "There. You are now on the road to recovery. Congratulations."

Scrooge sank to the ground and sat on the pavement. His ruin was indeed complete. He looked up at the Supervisor, broken, stunned, near lifeless. He moaned, as much to himself as to the phantom, "Now what, now what?"

"Believe me, Mr. Scrooge," said the Supervisor in sincerity, "we know what we're doing in our department, our little scheduling snafus aside. You'll recover from these setbacks with a greater understanding of what is of value in this world, and what is not."

"I have nothing left!" he shouted. "What is there of value for me now?"

"There is one thing," she reminded him, "although I am speaking quite apart from my official capacity right now. You still have the invitation to your nephew's house. I suggest you take him up on it and soak up some of his hospitality. Play some Scattergories, maybe watch the Grinch on television. You need to reconnect with the persuns around you, and Fred's would be a good place to start. It's been a pleasure serving you, Mr. Scrooge, and again, I apologize about last night." The Supervisory Spirit put her clipboard under her arm and without apparent effort receded into the background and disappeared.

So, with no other course of action apparent to him, Scrooge did as the Supervisory Spirit advised. He managed to hitch a ride from a truck driver hauling a load of frozen turkeys, and within a short time he was knocking on his nephew's front door. And he tried to enjoy himself with Fred and his wife, although the taste of "humble pie" was new and not wholly agreeable to him.

Over time, Scrooge worked hard to learn the lessons that his misfortunes were supposed to teach him, and in the end he succeeded. As he worked to rebuild his company, he learned the value of friendship and cooperation (mainly the friendship of bankers and industry insiders who helped him get back on his feet). He learned the value of giving, especially to the politicians who would protect his interests. And he learned that he was not alone in the world, and so paid more attention to his public image.

Finally, as a result of the intercession of the spiritual facilitators, Scrooge made certain to follow the exact letter of their teachings (if not their true intent) as it served him best, for he was fearful of undergoing more spiritual therapy or traveling with the ill-bred Ghost of Christmas Present ever again.